# THE MAN
## WHO BOUGHT HIS OWN DEATH

# THE MAN
## WHO BOUGHT HIS OWN DEATH

BERTHA LOPEZ GIRALDO

Library of Congress Control Number:          2019907456

HARDBACK:                 978-1-7337014-6-4
PAPERBACK:                978-1-7337014-5-7
EBOOK:                    978-1-7337014-7-1

Ordering Information:

For orders and inquiries, please contact:
1-888-404-1388
www.goldtouchpress.com
book.order@goldtouchpress.com


Printed in the United States of America

Translated from Spanish by Louise and Channing Horner

Composition by Diego L Sarmiento

To my sister Lucy,
my husband Diego,
and in loving memory of
my parents and brothers.

# The Man Who Bought His Own Death

Every afternoon, he returned disappointed to the country where he had had the misfortune to be born, a country in upheaval that gave no importance to moral values and where respect for human life was worth less than a penny.

He didn't remember exactly how many résumés he had presented to so many and such diverse businesses or the number of times he had waited in different Ministries, where almost always after many evasions and calls they changed the subject.

He came to the sad conclusion that without "connections" or some important influence his knowledge as a Business Administrator would not be recognized. That reality led him to pessimism, to long walks through the city without a fixed goal, and to long sleepless nights. As the months went by, he chose to visit private businesses, employment agencies, to which the desperate resorted and where long lines formed for an interview. He tried tempting newspaper ads, and finally everything turned out to be a fraud.

He stopped in parks full of unemployed people, places that were packed with lazy and needy people, with street urchins ruined by addiction that was their only stimulus to survive.

Beggars and more beggars crossed the nearby streets— on the sidewalks, at the entrances of restaurants, at the exits of theaters, and even beneath bridges.

The beggars were a scourge in the city. There were many who pursued by hunger behaved illegally; they snatched wallets, they begged menacingly. Lines of people filled the sidewalks when an ad seeking a skilled worker appeared. It was distressing to see so many skilled people for the few opportunities to work—scant hope in the face of such misery. The atmosphere was choking him. The economic situation of the country increased his distress since the main streets seemed desolate with numerous business premises vacant, some covered in dust and others disintegrating.

It seemed as if a destroying hand had stopped there, destroying past splendor. A crisis in the economy reflected in everything. Fear and despair seized him. He was certain that everything was the result of the damned war between the government and the guerrillas. A pitiful gash opened up, it was a wound, a feeling of numbness that went along capturing everyone, even when some appeared unaffected.

In all its corners the city offered only insecurity; armed assault could happen in any street, on the bus, in a taxi, in an elevator. Bank robbers managed to block the streets while they did their deed.

He had nothing to fear because he had nothing to lose; he had already lost it all. Nevertheless, he felt that day after day his patience was falling apart in the face of his struggle.

This was the space in which Alfred Medina's life unfolded. Failure and disillusionment were seen in his body and in his face; his clothing was beyond old, ragged with the genuine shine of having been washed and ironed too many times; his uncut hair as well as his sickly pallor and poet's beard gave him a favorable look to the eyes of someone who would change his destiny.

Disillusioned as the most tormented being in the world, that night he went into the Central Bar. Grisly thoughts seized him—mugging, robbery, death. What an unleashed hurricane, how illogical his thoughts were!

The Central Bar was at the corner of Altamira and Altagracia; it had the same noisy atmosphere as all bars but with very particular differences—among waves of smoke and murmuring moved the most dissimilar characters: the ambitious, cruel, and miserly millionaire; the eccentric and spendthrift; the insurance broker; the disheveled poet, haggard and surely hungry; the crook and the tramp who try to hide their misfortunes; the skillful vendor of emeralds; the shady drug dealer; the failed gambler who mentally curses his hands, the unknowing cause of his misery. The music at night was not thunderous and allowed conversation; the tangos were the most eagerly awaited: "... I dragged through this world the shame of having been and the pain of not yet being..." "Kiss me, kiss me over and over..." And in the middle of this hubbub, the swaying and sometimes immodest "waitresses", some of them rivers of boredom and fatigue, subject in their old age to servicing men who exploited them mercilessly.

On all the tables that night, there was an abundance of whiskey, spirits, rum, and brandy, and in contrast there was in addition the smell of recently brewed coffee and a strong mixed aroma of liqueurs. Our character, under faint light, in the most hidden corner of the bar, was trying to cover with his hands a handy cup of coffee that he was drinking, sip by sip, with obvious nervousness.

When Fabio Estenoz approached his table with ease and class and asked to take a chair and use another for his elegant black briefcase, Alfred Medina felt timid and inhibited. It was not without good reason. With his inferiority complex hovering and convinced that at forty he already was a man prematurely aged by hunger and the mishaps of life, humiliated by his own destiny, he felt that he was a piece of human waste and that he should not socialize with anyone; he started to get up, but the new arrival said:

_Please don't leave._

And extending his hand effusively:

_My name is Fabio Estenoz. Please let me buy you a drink._

Alfred reciprocated, shaking his hand as he said:

_Alfred Medina at your service._

Their poor hands, without knowing it, had just sealed a cruel destiny.

Fabio Estenoz was good looking, pleasant, very mannerly, with an overwhelming personality, a characteristic of those who move in wealthy high society; he enjoyed making friends without regard to social standing. He went around to bars, frequented clubs sharing smiles and making friends. His thirty-eight years were a testimony to the life that he seemed to love dearly. Under that pleasant tone of his voice, the hours slipped by happily and peacefully. Unexpectedly, he asked Alfred:

_Do you want to go or can we continue talking? The night has barely begun._

Medina answered him deliberately:

_Your suggestion pleases me; I enjoy listening to you. Tell me, do you like poetry? I have on hand an anonymous funny story. It's not a poem, but I like it._
_I, too, like poetry. You have no idea how much I like it!_ answered Fabio.
_Let's hear the funny story."

While the murmuring of voices rose in a swell throughout the large café, Medina spoke deliberately:

_"I have no fixed course, nor do I want one. I'm not following anyone, nor am I waiting for anyone. And since no one is awaiting my arrival, it's all the same to me if I arrive today, tomorrow, or any other day."_

They continued talking of poems, poets, and of their life. They brought up the lives of some of them. It was odd; they had the same preferences and were acquainted with the majority of the well-known poets. The conversation at one point centered on the "evil poets"—Baudelaire, Voltaire, and others; then on poets who had committed suicide; they spoke of Lugones, that marvelous Argentinian poet who committed suicide in 1938. And, oddly, they both knew by heart his poem "The Song of Distress":

> "I was walking alone and silent/ Because you were far away;/ And that night I was writing to you,/ when around the desolate house/ horror dragged its sinister outfit."

They discussed other topics, especially lurid ones about women, men, and politics. Under the powerful influence of liquor, happiness returned fleetingly to Alfred's life. He forgot about his clothing that showed him to be a classic pauper and in spite of that saw his happy childhood and a reliable and well-balanced man. For his part, during the hours of constant cordial conversation Fabio became acquainted with and took in some of Alfred's misfortunes.

_Your problems are so small, my friend_ he said, _so small that I can almost assure that you are "drowning in a glass of water," you are becoming bitter unfairly._

They celebrated with laughter. They drank to life, peace, and poetry. Fabio's voice, pleasant, manly, deep, musical, with perfect diction, murmured several parts of poems in prose with brilliant and enviable memory. The harmony and similarity between the two was such that they seemed to be brothers or old friends. When hours had gone by and the night was much advanced, Estenoz handed a card to Alfred, and while they said goodbye, he told him,

_Medina, don't forget; I believe your life can change!_

Back in his room, the effects of the liquor had almost disappeared, or at least that was the impression Alfred had. He thought for a long time about that strange friend that destiny had brought him and skeptically concluded that it was a fleeting friendship without lasting importance. He felt ashamed of his deplorable circumstances; he reflected on his years of studying. What good was it to be a business manager if the city was not only overflowing with them but also

with other professionals as competent as he was—
lawyers, engineers, economists, who had a multiplicity
of needs and sometimes drove taxis or emigrated to
other countries. The cruel reality was to continue the
struggle. The immediate one—solve his problems, the
most urgent being to pay the months of rent that he
owed his landlady.

With rapid, nervous movements he looked in his jacket,
in his pants pockets, in his misshapen wallet for the card
that his casual friend had just given him. He found it in
his old overcoat and while he pulled it out of his papers
a strange package that filled him with curiosity fell
on the floor. It contained—what a surprise!— barely
folded and wrapped in toilet paper, twenty 50,000-peso
bills. When? At what point had Fabio Estenoz put that
quantity of money in the pocket of his faded overcoat? It
could have been no one else but his unexpected friend.
Later on, he would know it for sure.

Ten o'clock in the morning found him submerged in the
sweet feeling of a dream, but he kept asking himself:

_Am I mistaken? Could it be the product of my
imagination? A hallucination perhaps?_

Instinctively he looked towards the nightstand. No,
he had not deceived himself; there within the reach

of his hand were the bills that he could feel, squeeze, smell; they symbolized, grand, the repayment of a few days, temporary peace, a hope, his brief freedom from the implacable landlady who had threatened to throw everything out onto the street.

Never did anyone love a million pesos as Alfred did on that unforgettable morning. He felt that he loved the peculiar odor of those bills, their seals, the signatures that gave them validity and that he examined carefully. How beautiful they were! How he loved, without knowing them, their printers and those who had signed them to make them valid! He loved the hands in whose possession they had been before they came to his. And lastly, with tears of happiness and exhaustion, he came to love also the unusual friend who surely had been the author of such a magnificent gift.

The value of some bills that turned up in a pocket of a shabby overcoat can be the cause of a very human transformation. In the yellowed mirror of his room, he saw eyes—his eyes—made bigger by hope, shining and anxious because of what he had just been through.

What a wretched human vileness we men have to experience because of money and for money. Why does a man have to candidly live to pursue happiness in material things? Why do we have to live condemned by ambition? Why can't we find happiness within ourselves? Sometimes a man sets up harsh goals hard to reach, that is why happiness becomes a metaphor, a chimera, greed becomes dominant, economic crisis lashes us and we enclose ourselves on a shadowy maze as in Alfred's case.

_Oh beautiful lord money!_ Medina exclaimed as he smiled and happily caressed the bills that were giving him his life back.

The offices of Fabio Estenoz were right in the heart of city, in the Carrier Building, fifth floor. His name stood out of the door and below it a list of properties: La Amelia, California, Valencia, Petruska, among others.

After crossing through several rooms where employees of both genders were at work, Medina had himself announced to Fabio. Little by little, a strange terror began to take hold of him and in his mind soft voices spoke to him. What if he refused to speak to see him? What if he didn't acknowledge the conversation he had with him, now three days ago? A feeling of terror invaded him; a thousand conjectures and reflections squeezed his soul. After all, he is rich and I am poor; he a wide river and I a muddy stream; he a millionaire and I a shameful wretch. He would have to repay the million pesos that he had already put to use; he was wearing a tie, new shoes, and a simple suit also purchased in an inexpensive shop. But the truth is that he was glimmeringly neat.

Twenty minutes later Fabio Estenoz received him in his private office. Immediately Alfred noticed that Estenoz had fresh ideas and that he was overflowing with kindness and optimism. He shook his benefactor's hand firmly and with his most pleasant smile went to sit in a spacious armchair. Without looking at him directly, he began to stammer:

_Three nights ago, Mr. Estenoz, I received from you..._
_Forget about that,_ he interrupted. _My friend, think about today, about this minute._
_But it was you,_ insisted Alfred. _You gave me..._
_No need to tell me. I remember it all perfectly._
_Mr. Estenoz, what I want and need is to work,_ Medina stated vehemently. _For that reason I have come to ask your help._

Again he cut off his sentence,

_I was expecting you, my friend. I want to propose that you collaborate with me. It happens that I am needing someone like you, and now is the time for you to show your qualifications and skill as a business administrator. To begin with, you will go with me to some of my properties; you will advise me on many things. I need a genuinely trustworthy man, and I believe, without fear of being mistaken, that you can be that person and that, if you plan to, you will do a great job._

For a moment, Alfred Medina had fleeting thoughts and memories. The voice of his dead mother, like a murmur, sounded sweetly in his ears:

_"Son, don't forget that 'mines with so much gold do not exist" and "Everything has its reason."_

But as the saying goes, "Necessity has no law" and "Opportunity knocks only once." Alfred had no other option than to accept gratefully the opportunity that he was being offered, not without giving thanks in various ways to the person who with such altruism was giving him a hand in such a difficult moment of his life.

Estenoz treated his employees with great familiarity, but at the same time with such refined honor and graciousness that no one dared to show disrespect. In his offices, on his properties, anywhere he went, he was treated like what he appeared to be—an important gentleman. At first Alfred began to move at the side of his employer with definite timidity; he still was carrying around in his personality the robes of poverty, and that inferiority complex in which poverty is cloaked still devastated him. Months later the income from his work brought him security and comfort. He began to enjoy life. The idea of suicide gradually faded away.

With what accuracy Fabio Estenoz had predicted his future!

From the lips of his father, Alfred learned from childhood the standards of uprightness and honesty. For that reason, he was quick to serve efficiently and nobly the one who had healed his wounds, that Samaritan who had stretched forth his hands to keep him from drowning; the one who without being aware of it, possibly by a chance of fate, had become the protector of an anonymous poor wretch.

Medina took upon himself the task of making the rounds of all the properties, particularly of those devoted to the best crops. He purchased several books about them, studied with admirable dedication and persistence. Soon he was an expert on the subject and an efficient administrator. Fabio Estenoz in his work contract had given him a flattering and important title: "Representative and General Administrator".

Probably because his benefactor had spoken with praise of Medina, or simply because they supposed that a person would have to be very knowledgeable to get to such a position, all the staff members whether in the office or in the field clearly regarded him and treated him with respect. The majority of the crops were to be examined by the General Representative. Likewise, all purchases of machinery required his approval. So it was that he approved most of the business decisions. In a year he had taken such thorough possession of his job and all its parts that he had become the stem and sap of that business. Even though his main headquarters was in the capital, where he had rented and furnished an elegant but modest apartment, he enjoyed visiting each week the favorite property of his protector—La Petruska. The house, built with great luxury and meticulousness, had more than can be imagined: comfortable bedrooms with private baths, huge windows through which the sun shone abundantly; the red tiled roofs which were hardly visible because they were planted with orchids of the most diverse colors, gave "La Petruska" an exotic and dazzling appearance. The San Luis River flowed calmly through the marshes and gave the whole place a calm, serene feeling. The surrounding gardens were a fantasy of fountains for birds and waterfalls that provided musical murmurs in the silence of the countryside.

Inside, the furniture was lavish—in some places, Louis XV pieces framed with velvet drapes; in other corners, beautiful Queen Ann chairs and armchairs; a huge fireplace, a beautiful piano, and classical paintings covering the walls. Everything shone fresh and clean; in one wing of the mansion there was a small chapel, beautiful with an immense Christ in the center illuminated with the colors of the stained glass windows; there were also some pictures of scenes from the Bible on one wall, memorial stones with the ashes of his grandparents, of his parents, and of the only brother of Fabio Estenoz. Leaving the Chapel, on the right, there was a long hallway full of photographs of himself and his family in various countries, on airplanes, on ships, with the names of all of the places that had been visited and the dates.

Among the eccentricities of Fabio Estenoz was that of keeping alive the memory of his ancestors, seen in those photos of his people in earlier times which caused sudden shivers before the insistence of their serious expressions. The closets of the house were full of all sorts of luxurious dresses that were aired every week as if they were used frequently; they were shaped with astonishing exactness; others contained complete gentlemen's outfits perfectly organized. Nobody dared to desecrate or to ask the reason for that whim of maintaining with such care all those things belonging to people who had gone away never to return. It was Fabio's decree that everything that belonged to those he had lost through death should continue in that artificial and mysterious life. His father's library was dusted daily; his musical collections were put away in special pieces of furniture, meticulously as if he were alive and with great care. Everything in the house would seem to be unrest upon a certain movement except for two real people who needed to be taken care of: Fabio Estenoz and Alfred Medina, and that by chance. The rest were people on the "staff", trusted workers with many years of service there who fulfilled their routine job of keeping the rooms up to date for beings who only passed through in the shadows. No one commented on adverse conditions, it was so normal that everyone seemed to be filled with his ideas; on several occasions there was heard the complaint of one employee or another because there had been a delay in putting out the absent master's favorite music or in organizing his library.

Rarely was Fabio Estenoz sad or apathetic. A joy that seemed to be sincere and spontaneous accompanied him constantly; he took delight in all the simple aspects of nature—the normal liveliness of a calf, which he gathered into his arms with particular tenderness;

the sonorous impact of hail and rain when they fell heavily on the roofs, windows, and trees; he smiled with the first rose buds, with the colorfulness of the orchids or with the whirlwind of dry yellow leaves that always brought along waves of sand; the hurricane that roared furiously on winter nights and that caused the eucalyptus and pine trees to knock into each other left him nearly immobile from emotion, almost holding his breath before this natural phenomenon. In addition, Fabio Estenoz loved painting and theater, and one of his greatest pleasures was the season of international theater that came to the city each year. He was thrilled by the works of Shakespeare, especially *Hamlet*, which he had seen several times and of which he knew several passages by heart. He admired Kafka and savored French theater during the years he lived in Paris; *The Humane Voice* of Jean Cocteau with its sickly bitter flavor captivated him. He admired Goethe when he read *Werther*.

It was strange, he felt an uncontrollable attraction to what was tragic; he loved classical painting, he had a collection of biographies of almost all the painters, he read and re-read the tormented life of Van Gogh. In addition to his literary hobbies, he was a weapons enthusiast and had a full collection of them; one of his entertainments was target shooting. So it didn't seem strange to Alfred to accompany his boss in his entertainments in the afternoon after their business appointments, at the same time taking an intensive course in target shooting. This with the "noble intention", as he said, of learning to appreciate and enjoy such an "important" sport. From time to time, Alfred accompanied him while Estenoz explained the workings of some of his recently purchased weapons and pontificated on their use:

_Accuracy, my friend, is decisive in a good shooter. If you hesitate or are afraid, you are lost_

Lost, Alfred thought. Lost in what? If I'm a peace-loving man, I have no enemies, my hands are incapable of being raised to down even a small animal that threatens me. He allowed him to reflect at length and to express fully his interest in weapons and hunting, which privately he considered "innocent obsessions." After a few months, one morning Fabio Estenoz said jubilantly:

_You turned out to be such a good student, such a good shooter, so accurate, so precise, that I am proud of you_

Medina replied:

_Thank you. I have learned one more thing in life and, as you say, something very useful. We live in a warlike country, but I will never use this skill in hunting, because as you know, I love animals, as violent as some of them may be. I would be incapable of treating a single one of them violently_

_I know that, of course, my dear friend Alfred. You would even allow yourself to be killed by a cat if it attacked you_

And he laughed uproariously, marking the end of the scene.

# The Man Who Bought His Own Death

It is a cruel irony of life that a person comes to know himself when circumstances and life accuse him of dishonorable conduct. I need to tell about my life, scrutinize all the corners of my past, search myself out in my childhood, in my adolescence, in all the hours that make up my existence; in spite of everything I think that there are moments in which I think I am not me, but I am me, even if I can't see myself in a mirror. I feel the lines of my face and I know who I am. The truth is that if I had a mirror, I wouldn't want to see myself; I want to maintain the image of the person I was. I exist! I am here, confronting to my fate! I am Alfred Medina! I spend time pondering day after day within the four walls of my prison cell. Yes, I am a prisoner! I, who love freedom, I who tremble with love and goodness for every being.

I am in this place with my blood poisoned, my spirit destroyed by misfortune, with my best feelings torn to shreds, cut down like trees after a hurricane. Now there is only anguish and disillusionment in my heart. Because of the overcrowding in the prison, I share the depressing cell where I am, for only a few days they told me. My companion is a twenty-four-year-old guerilla who has been fighting since he was fourteen. His tales are dramatic. He has told me his tragic story, and we have established between us a brief but unforgettable friendship. His life and mine share a relationship, a story. Even though they don't have the same appearance, they are united by grief and they have the same roots. The guerillas attacked his home in the countryside, cruelly and fiercely assassinating his parents and two of his brothers. They carried off everything that his family had attained with the struggle of their labor. They gave him a gun, and his life has taken place among bullets and death, in the midst of disastrous drug trafficking and the wickedness of the atmosphere around him. He is well aware of the bitterness of isolation and the evil maneuvers of those who captured him and dragged him into this life; he's a deserter, fed up with disgrace and hoping for a pardon or an amnesty to vindicate himself. We have talked a lot; I have listened to him eagerly, and he asks me:

_When all is said and done, friend, I don't understand. What is war?_

_War is the scourge we have had for many years. To my mind, it is the confrontation with daily life; the chasm between those above and those below; the empty refrigerator of the shamefully poor; the frayed and shiny clothes of the wretched; the worm-eaten soles on the shoes of poor students; the necessary wandering around of the unemployed with vain hopes; it is knowing that millions of young people cannot attend a university for lack of economic means and that they see their aspirations frustrated before the wall of poverty. War is the bus and taxi drivers who travel the streets violently, expressing their brutality; it's the millionaire or the executive who with total lack of respect in their dazzling automobiles run down anyone who crosses their path because they own everything and have every right; war is the corrupt employee who raises barriers in the office; ministers and highly placed civil servants who are inaccessible to little people like me, who have been trying for a year to get a simple meeting with one of them, even when I gave up my ambitions. War is the humiliations that the citizen or small businessman suffers before the financial enterprises when he is in search of a loan; war is usury and the high interest rates charged by the banks, which leads to expropriation and to the loss of a home for thousands of families. War is the lack of awareness, the hate, the contempt, the blindness towards the deprived; it is the unprecedented taunt of businessmen who unfurl big expensive pages in the newspapers with ridiculous bargains; it is the lie that prevails, impertinent duplicity; the lack of medicines for the poor and their lack of health care_

I paused briefly, but my companion urged me to continue.

_War_ I repeated, _is jails full of people who become trash because there is no societal plan to redeem them; it's the extensive capital of the privileged that is inherited from generation to generation and which is fed by the forced inequality and ignorance of the people; war is street muggers and the abundant white-collar thieves who abound in the upper crust of society; war is abandoned women and those who without any hope struggle and work silently under the burden of responsibilities in a suffocating chauvinist atmosphere—the women who gripped by hunger and need give themselves on dark streets; war is the destitute and reviled old people and children; it is those who are displaced by violence, rejected, and excluded.

My friend, I tell you it will end when the people speak and their voice is not the wound from which they are bleeding_

After a brief silence, my cellmate admitted emphatically:

_I respect your opinions, and I admire the courage and accuracy of your assessment. I can assure you that you are clearly aware of the universal condition_

One morning, silently, without any explanation, I was moved to another place. I never found out anything more about my friend the guerilla who longed to vindicate himself. From my new cell I hear moans, swearing, curses that make the hours longer and deeper, the nights blacker and more tedious; I can see the arms of prisoners waving their hands in desperation. I hear groans, cries, and shouts, tenuous prayers. There come odors of excrement, of urine, of sweat, of damp clothing; rumors of protest, plans for attacks, clamoring for uprisings. At other times, firecrackers and sometimes roaring and crowds. Twice a day I hear the train, swift and steady, going by. Its long and penetrating lament has become familiar to me; it is a message, a promise, a hope. Will it happen that someday that I will again go through the countryside among endless rows of trees, by the craggy mountains, in a speeding train that, like this one, will fill my hours and shout my loss of freedom?

My regular companions in my loneliness are the flies. All this that surrounds me, that chokes me, that imprisons and torments me is their world and my world, our world. Sometimes, tired of their rhythmical flying in the gloomy space of my cell, they gather around me and spin around my head, as if they wanted to penetrate my eyes in order to wound them. They can regain their freedom just by going through the bars of my enclosure. Fly towards the open sky, towards the light, towards life, towards infinite space; but the disgusting things search out the manure in the courtyards and come back to keep me company. Irony of life! I mock them by covering my head with the coarse blanket that I have and after buzzing around and looking in vain for my face and hair, they go off just a little way to mate. When I uncover myself, I see them on the walls, on the rough bars of my bunk, on the floor, everywhere, black, moving; they exasperate me, they drive me crazy, I go after them tirelessly; I smash their bodies, full of eggs, but the next day my space is invaded by others, as if the mental punishment they inflict on me were nothing. How I hate them!

One day, in the corner of my cell, there appeared there appeared the head of a little rat, timid and trembling at first. It had fresh, shiny hair, tiny transparent ears with a slight color of pink at the erect and vibrating tips, eyes that gave warning, lively and quick and seeming to take in even the most hidden things, a swaying little body with delicate extremities. It was a pleasure to see how in the darkness of the night, guided by its instinct and a flickering ray of moonlight, it fearfully shared my humble supper. Some days later, it walked around my cell with the certainty of a model on the runway. My tiny visitor, adorable at first, became bullying and brash; it brought along a legion of companions, some old, others repulsive, some whose bodies were white, others black, all repulsive. That's when I decided to end my friendship with the little creature. One morning I put a large stopper, a bare ear of corn, in the opening of its cave; it was a simple impediment but one which resisted the sharp teeth. From that morning, another secret sadness has been added to my life—the sadness of no longer seeing the clear eyes of my little rat in the moonlight.

I have been a good man, in the full sense of the word; that's the way I see myself. Determined to work out a ne w life for myself, with the hope of beginning to live in spite of my forty years. But fate has brutally torn me apart with absolutely no respect; that's why I am in a jail, a victim and not guilty. I hate violence and I condemn the day it came in through the black door of my disaster. Thoughts that want to break out swim in my head, and I say to myself words that are dictated by my conscience: Keep going! Don't stop! You are innocent!

Thanks to the kindness of my jailer who gives me paper and pencil, I can write these truths, my defense before the judges and the world, because as the great Spanish writer Ortega y Gasset said, "I am myself and my circumstances, and if I don't rescue them I can't rescue myself."

No one can visit. But who would, I ask myself, if my only friend was my enemy and, besides, he's dead? I am in solitary confinement, disconnected from the world outside, in the hands of a court-appointed lawyer, the only one to whom I have a right. Perhaps he will be helped by my digressions, the story of my life with Fabio Estenoz. Let him draw his own conclusions, judge my position freely, without requiring me to accept situations in which I don't belong.

Being in prison is to feel that the threads of our life have been permanently broken; it is to have an uncertain and variable future, to travel through the past at a constant gallop between the hours that are gone and those of the present. The cell becomes a permanent stage set with only one character; the other actors are the shadows that are moved by the strings of the imagination. The persistent desire to be removed from this circumstance becomes a permanent interior cry, an obsessive conviction: I am innocent; I am innocent! And the voices bang against the silent walls.

In order to allay this obsession, I set myself to remembering my childhood: my spirit flew over the paths I had taken; I went in search of my past and saw myself at the age of nine, with a fervent look and a pure heart; in the garden of my house I laid to rest the sweet dog Kazan who died of old age. I saw my friends who kindly helped me with such a bitter task. We covered him with heartfelt crying. It was the best homage we could give to our faithful companion. My mother sowed seeds on the grave and a beautiful rosebush grew; on day I wanted to pull it up to look for the mystery, but she stopped me with these words that I will never forget, "Don't be senseless, are you going to destroy your dog's soul?" Ever since then, rosebushes evoke my strongest feeling. My father had a beautiful marker made with the unforgettable poem of Lord Byron for his beloved dog Boatswain:

> Near this Spot
> are deposited the Remains of one
> who possessed Beauty without Vanity,
> Strength without Insolence,
> Courage without Ferocity,
> and all the virtues of Man without his Vices.

Of all my memories, those of my childhood are now my present: when we were children, how slow December was in coming; the books were forgotten at home and it was time for the trip from the city to the country; our house had white walls and a red roof; from the gate you could see the carnations and poppies bowing to the lilies; our screaming tortured the immense ears of the countryside; our laughter, clear childish laughter, carried our new feelings to the old roads, to the woods, and to the country people, simple friends who knew how to play the guitar skillfully and who sang Christmas carols and folk songs; I remember that one day, with my cousins, we demolished the little bridge of the Río Blanco that was essential for those of our household that was on the high part of the mountain; afterwards we had no fear because when our mother arrived outraged and ready to punish us, Father stopped her with these wise words, "Let them alone, dear; remember that it is December, the time when the spirit gets out of control and children become wild colts."

My childhood with my sweet beautiful little grandmother—she told us surprising stories, she got my cousins and me to thinking, and we were all happy; listening to her stories was better than reading any children's book; she told us about the crazy people in the town who were running around loose and who were not as dangerous as the ones that are currently invading us; we were astounded hearing her, and for our mother she was the "be still" and "stay there" that she wanted. "There was a crazy man," Grandmother would begin, "strong and tall, who ran through the streets screaming in his thunderous voice, 'I am Napoleon Bonaparte' and another who, dressed in a long loose coat, raised his eyes heavenward and acted like a monk with a huge thick rosary whose beads he counted continually; the children of those days shouted at him, 'Jacinto! You old married man!' That would make him furious, and he would brandish a club that he carried hidden and if some of them got to close they were injured." Grandmother explained that in those days there were no insane asylums out in the country; for that reason there were so many crazy people running loose, and if a wealthy family had the misfortune to have someone insane, they were obliged to take him to the capital. Grandmother's tales were so traditional of the region and she told them with such conviction and intensity that sometimes they instilled fear in us, particularly if we listened to them at night; she knew that the stories of Little Red Riding Hood and the wolf were no longer suitable for us. That's why she put such effort into strange tales that would leave us anxious and amazed. Grandmother continued: "the coffin that crosses in front of country people at midnight as they come home late from work; the light that traveled along the Río Grande when she was a child; the story of the witches who meet in the treetops; the footsteps that were heard in the halls and the sharp knock on the dining room table at two in the morning; the phantom bus that went by at one in the morning with no driver; the garden ghosts and the spine-chilling cemeteries"— so many tales of those days. Once we asked how many years old she was, and she told us vehemently, "Never tell how many years old you are; you can answer when they ask, How many do you need?"

Those who are absent from us wander around during our nights of insomnia. The faces seem clearer, more spontaneous, more real, even those that death and time cover with their thick veils; they seem ruinous and certain. Insomnia is the magic mirror of memories; that's why when I recalled my mother's face the inevitable feelings that turned into reality with her permanent absence emerged. Seeing her suffering on her bed, at 58 years of age and apparently healthy, full of hope and desire to live, opened in me a wound that never heals.

I remember a morning when my mother's condition had already become too weak that she asked me, as a good Catholic, that I request last rites for her; quickly, obedient to all her wishes, I immediately got to the streets that separated me from a nearby church. I remember it perfectly. It was eleven in the morning; I got to the door of priest's house and rang the bell three times. Impatient at the door because nobody answered, I tried another three rings. Finally a maid appeared at a window.

_What do you need?_ she asked rudely.

_Please, the priest! It's urgent; my mother is seriously ill and needs him! It's not far from here, please!_ I repeated in desperation.

The maid closed the window and after a while returned to tell me coldly and with indifference,

_Didn't you see the sign on the door? Read it: I provide services only at the hours indicated_

Exasperated, I reprimanded her,

_But, woman, what kind of an answer is that? How can a minister of God be so indifferent? Call him, please!_ I insisted.

The woman closed the window again, went into the inner part of the house, and returned a few minutes later to tell me scornfully,

_Father cannot help you at this time; come back in the afternoon_

As if those who are dying could wait! I felt the blood burning in my veins; my fists turned to stone and I shouted at the heartless servant,

_Tell that heartless man that I didn't come asking favors, that you were mistaken, that I am here bringing a pile of money for his church! Tell him that and see how quickly he puts his life in danger by flying down the steps_

I said all that as loud as I could, intending for him to hear it. And it worked, because as I was headed home again I looked back and there, on the balcony, was the Vicar with his fists raised menacingly; I raised mine in return.

Then came back to mind all the incidents and situations regarding some "ministers of the Church"—the one who said his Mass only for "Ministers of State" and who humiliated poor women and men in ponchos who dared to set foot in the Mass of the privileged. I recalled the one who said he did not accept alms of less than a specified amount; the one who wanted to wear large gold rings or any other jewelry and would receive them with pleasure in the name of God; the same one who became swollen in pride with a widow who moved him by giving him the only thing her husband had left her— the gold rings that symbolized their marriage. I recalled the priest and teacher who caused all his students to fail; they pulled the childish prank of filling his car with rotten tomatoes. He reacted saying:

_Those who filled my car with rotten tomatoes, I forgive their wickedness in the name of God, because He forgives all; to those heartless ones I, like Jesus, turn the other cheek and, like Him, I forget all the evil they do me_

What extraordinary reasoning that would be if it were sincere! Then, furious, he drew a breath and with a contorted face continued,

_But putting aside what there is of God and bringing forth what I am as a man, I say and I repeat to those scoundrels that they are a bunch of sons of bitches!_

I remembered Eça de Queiroz when I read him and got to know him at an early age in *The Sin of Father Amaro*. I thought about Jesus, the philosopher, wise, noble, just, humble, companion of all the destitute who long for eternal equality and glory. How useless his sacrifice was! How useless his beautiful teaching. If he were to return, he would whip the new vendors in the temples, those who distort his teaching and ruin the work of the true apostles. But it is also true that if Jesus returned he would be crucified again. The human heart is so disconcerting!

In the same way, on those nights of insomnia and nightmares my father and the memory of him march past. A shadow among the shadows. He had cinnamon-colored skin and a kindly face. I saw him as tall as the mountains, as strong as the trees in the forest. He was convinced, as a blind man believes in his night, that his religion and his politics were the only means of salvation; having a different opinion never persuaded him, as he affirmed in a little book that he published, along with several others. As child I saw his political struggles, always based on the divine. I carry in my heart as a truth that simple man with big ideas, noble, kindly, in whom I saw the perfect model for my conduct; I have never been able to understand how such noble feelings were turned aside by false and unhealthy prophets who, I swear, were not able to destroy my love for him nor my admiration of his nobility and his great spirit of piety, a thorough-going philanthropist. But my father, in addition to what I have just said, was an outstanding writer and poet. When I began to think and pay attention to what was around men, I smelled the fragrance of fresh ink that came from the books he had written, closed up in a room of the big old house; they were piled up to the ceiling. He made big tours through the little towns in our region to sell and publicize his books personally.

After many months my father would return tanned by the sun of the southern jungles. He would tell me about his adventures with the Indians, about the slaves in the Arana household, about the large rivers he crossed, and about his dreams and about death that, under the influence of extremely high fevers, appeared to threaten that he would never get out of those places. From those experiences came his books *Eastern Jungles, Over the Caquetá, The Countess of the Valley.*

How I miss the presence of my father with his friendly word and what a sense of emptiness there is with the absence of his strong hands to show the way! His life was broken and I was left adrift like a boat without a rudder.

Nostalgia for my father sank deeply into my spirit and I think I carry it in my soul as an inescapable part of my inheritance; my childhood years are saturated with his wisdom and sound judgment; I remember the time I took him the grades from my teacher, who had added at the end, a little sarcastically, the following sentence:

Note: "They say he is a poet and that he's already in flight."

When I took them back to school signed, I saw with amazement how my father had answered the teacher:

"If he were a poet and if he were flying / As the illustrious cherubim flies / Piercing with the brush of their wings / The beautiful lace of the clouds, / Then I would be happy / And would never succumb to defeat, / If piercing the heavy dark clouds / The young man were consistent with your note."

I recalled one of his poems that he taught me when I was very young and that he recited frequently remembering the trip that he made with his older son to put him in a hospital in the capital, where he died:

"How sad to see the horizon / When the train rolls across the plain! / My poor heart is throbbing / Draining the cup of bitterness."

I remembered childhood vacations when my father used to take me to the countryside with which I became familiar; I was delighted enjoying milking time; with wide eyes I took in the birth of a calf; my little hands offered the cattle corn, salt, and brown sugar. One night I got out and slept several hours on the warm chest of a cow until my parents came and got me; I enjoyed the affable company of Lightning and Thunderbolt, two harmless old horses who went to sleep when you mounted them and were all we had at that time for getting to town. My father told how he had purchased them at the market, giving them the names of Lightning and Thunderbolt because the day he bought them they were restless and lively, headstrong and eager to head off running; later he found out that in that market they used to put hot pepper on the horses' tails so they would sell well. In any case, I loved them and for me horses are sacred, with their sad eyes, their heavy long eyelashes, and their manes blowing in the wind, with their huge face that radiates intelligence. I love all horses, and it grieves me deep inside when they are mistreated or driven to death, overworked and worn out.

At that time, my view of life was very pure and transparent. At night I listened to the group of workers who, seated in a circle in front of the fireplace, began their stories and fables told in simple language but with great emotion; for an adolescent like me, it was a pleasure to listen to them even though my eyes were closing with sleepiness:

"The one legged one that went out alone on dark nights. Dead people who walked suspended above the earth, in the early morning mist. The coffin on the road that crossed in front of drunken country folks. The priest who had died years before but could still be heard saying Mass at midnight in the little village church. The light that went down the Río Grande on moonlit nights. The woman who dove into the river but previously had thrown her child into the raging water and often was heard to say, 'I threw him here; here is where I will find him.' The woman's leg that swung back and forth like a pendulum in front of the wall of the big fireplace. The abandoned house at the side of the road, the 'hanged man's house,' lighted up sometimes by the devil and where the hanged man could be seen swinging back and forth with his tongue out. The soldier who in the only inn in town would go down the hall to the bathroom at two in the morning, awakening everyone with the sound of his boots and sword, but who disappeared when anyone came out to catch him."

The night passed slowly, and I continued reviewing my life, my loves. What a parade of beautiful women chained to my past! Lucrecia, divine, I was still feeling the warmth of her kisses, of her loving arms; Ligia, Nancy, Helena, and Gloria. I repeated the poem of the great poet of the sea, Héctor Pedro Blomberg: "the hundred women who loved me / have now forgotten me, captain."

How many names of women besieged my night, how many breasts, how many lips, how many beautiful eyes, how many curves, how many caresses! How many! And the boredom, the disappointments, and the betrayals. The betrayals—Magda, how beautiful she was and how sweet! Passion and attractiveness pulled me towards her. Like most of the women, from the beginning she wanted to take me to the altar; I incredulous, a confirmed distrustful person, had settled on the idea of not being tied to anyone; to be free like the wind, not to commit myself for any reason. My ardent passion and my sincere convincing words found a response in Magda. We went off to take advantage of our youth by loving each other to the point of worship. That year with her was beautiful. I came to be so accustomed to her adorable company and her exquisite presence that the mere thought of her absence tormented my soul. But one morning she announced overjoyed that she was going to have a child—"our child," she said over and over with tears of joy. My loving companion did not know that I was unable to produce a child. I left her peacefully one day, without reproach, without demands, without a scene, without even finding out who had caused the pregnancy. Poor Magda, who seemed to be so innocent, tried to trick me and lost; I know that I lived a false life with her and that I was totally naïve to believe in her. I promised myself never again to fall into an error that cause me so much grief; now I smile at overcoming that stage, but sometimes the scars hurt deeply.

All my life's struggles kept running chaotically through my imagination: that time when I set up a small industrial business with only the proceeds from some savings hoping for support from the government that "was said to favor" small industrialists; when I asked for their assistance, they told me they only made loans to those who had significant capital; at a critical moment, I had to call upon a "friend" who authorized some bank overdrafts. Ah! But only in exchange for my discretely slipping him a bundle of bills. I still feel disgust and shame; my struggle at that point was titanic and, more painfully, unsuccessful and futile. I ended up losing everything, always to the benefit of the powerful, of the capitalists; my money disappeared, my time was lost; several years' work went to fatten the account of one of those "personages" who manage our democratic countries; useless people, dim-witted, without merit; but with evil cunning and by obscure procedures I saw them changed overnight into influential owners of large estates, of sumptuous residences, just because they set out with a political current that brought everything along with it. It's sad and it causes disillusionment to think that the ambitions of many of our public figures, the political and religious battles are only for a personal financial gain that corrupts the generations seeing them; they transform power into a hereditary illness that is transmitted from father to son and whose result is centuries-old oligarchy—a hydrogen bomb, a sword of Damocles held over the ignorant and decent masses with no support and overwhelmed. Capitalism continues to reign in the world, and those who say they are fighting for the people are a bunch of impudent greedy folks with capital based on blood and sweat, the product of unfair extortion that causes revulsion and nausea. Meanwhile, the good people see themselves required to live hidden and fearful; the streets are dangerous, desolate, and there are abundant vacant premises with similar signs: "for sale," "for lease"— all faded by the sun and time. Streets, where formerly buyers and sellers swarmed about and where prosperity shone, now seem to have been destroyed by a hurricane.

# The Man Who Bought His Own Death

I remember life with Fabio Estenoz very well.

I am recalling most of it at the moment and looking for a crack where justice can penetrate and know, investigate, and be clear about it. Yes, I remember it perfectly from the very moment when I entered it through the doorway of his kindness. On one of my birthdays Fabio had given me a pistol and a complete set of ammunition, of which I used only a small quantity in brief practices of target shooting, at his constant request. He insisted that I should "practice" with that modern gadget that stayed in a case in the display cabinet in my room; I feared that at any moment the police would confiscate it from me on one of their frequent patrols that they carried out because of the recent violence; my fear of losing it, more than for the weapon itself, was because it was a gift from my benefactor. Every bit of his property and belongings was sacred for me.

As he was the patron of a poor man, few or almost none of his attitudes seemed strange or crazy to me. In front of strangers he treated me with a certain affected respect:

_Mr. Medina will take care of that problem. Mr. Medina will supervise the harvest of the crop because I will be out of the country at that time_

On the other hand, in private meetings, which took place almost always on special occasions (Christmas, New Year's, birthdays) when happiness sprang forth, Fabio Estenoz was no longer formal with me, and my name, like a mechanical toy, came galloping out of his mouth. Under the influence of alcohol, a different personality showed itself; he suffered unquestionably from a painful split personality that altered his happiness, changing it into disillusionment, boredom, and nostalgia; his change was as sudden as the derailing of a train or the transformation of a chrysalis or like the darkness when the light is turned off.

Politics was one of his favorite topics; his voice would unleash a string of insults against the "puppets" of the government:

_You don't understand,_ he said to me (as he placed his right hand on my shoulder). _You don't understand politics, but I will teach you my religion, which is the harshest and surest of politics_

_Do you want greatness, Alfred Medina? I will make you great like the steppes where my dreams dance, like the immense rocks against which I have uselessly dashed my thoughts. Do you want a true politics? A stoic politician? Look at me!_ he shouted, and while fixing his drunken eyes on my eyes simultaneously pounded his chest with his right hand and exclaimed loudly, _I am a president without a country, a minister without portfolio. And do you know why? Because I was not born a thief. Most politicians are the owners of unimaginable fortunes along with their supporters, a huge range of speculators who preach popular ideas, while those leaders of the majority parties only wish fervently that stronger and more powerful countries will invade us. All their howls and displays against interventionism are crass lies. Their arrogance is another farce to retain power; it's just a fantasy that they use to get votes, but they don't think about it when they mortgage the country, when they deposit huge sums in foreign banks, when they buy valuable properties, according to them for the general good. The real warrior is the people, not just through scientific and historical conviction, but rather through repugnance towards so many nations to which the system and their leaders have mercilessly led them_

And he continued ceremoniously, _My friend Medina, it will be better to wait until the politicians calm down so that it doesn't happen to them as it did to a bunch of atheists who seeing themselves in danger of death on a boat that was near sinking began to pray, and the captain shouted sarcastically, 'Shut up. Don't go and let God know you are on this boat.'_

I was delighted by those caustic comments from Fabio Estenoz, and we both laughed heartily at them, like two unworried, irresponsible, and almost cynical students.

On other occasions, he fell into philosophizing in a perhaps overwhelming way:

_It is sad to think, friend Medina, that at the very time that the people devoutly say the word 'politics' and suffer and struggle and almost die for it, those who eternally exploit it, those of the stripe of the politicians who preach it, do nothing but debase it, prostitute it to their own advantage. When will this monstrous farce end?_

And he answered his own question: _When man understands the scientific union of man to man_

With thunderous laughter, in the sharpness of which there bubbled an obvious feeling of rebellion against everything in current politics, Fabio concluded his attacks, in which he ridiculed himself, leaving me bewildered. I remained cautiously silent, which could be interpreted one way or the other, approving or disapproving.

And he continued: _What say you, friend, about the homage that is given among us to any politician seeking immortality? And what about the tribute to the idol of the moment? And what about the sudden changes of 'popular fury' that today praises and makes a god of a man and tomorrow vilifies and destroys him?_

He summarized his rosary of questions by summing it up:

_At the end of it all there is not, on the part of the masses, the much-praised public opinion, but rather feelings of innate vileness, an anxiousness for chains that crops up indecently, an overflowing of implacable and latent hunger and thirst, of bloody brutality, created and inculcated from our first steps, picked up in the environment and in the education of our peoples_

That's how Fabio rambled.

And I, his most fervent friend and servant, was also his sole audience, his packed town square, his applause. I must not hide it now; he was my orator, my best orator. His words were opening paths in my mind. My reasoning fell right in with his ideas. Unknown parts of my life were discovered, and in the majority of his words I thought I found wisdom and truth. He explained to me in detail almost all national and international political life, scrutinizing in his way, with certainty and preciseness, the major problems, even predicting economic situations that I saw come to pass with frightening accuracy in the course of those days. Once, on a wild night, of which there were many, I asked him unexpectedly:

_Fabio, do you believe in God?_

Thoughtful and sad, he looked at me and said:

_I believe in a universal God who created people who commit suicide, atheists, saints, and criminals. A God who creates but does not punish. A God 'beyond good and evil,' a God without religions_

_What do you mean without religions?_ I asked him. _But these are the walls of restraint and the hope of humankind_

_Religions cannot retrain passions_ he answered angry and domineering. _Religions are the indelible stamp of humanity_

Very quietly I commented: _Then how is vice to be restrained? On what does virtue rest?_

_Vice and virtue are the source of life, my friend Medina_

Totally astonished, I replied:

_Why? Why?_

_Because they were born with man. Nothing good can exist without something evil, just as in nature man does not exist without woman, or day without night. Besides, religions are for those who go along blindly through them not knowing with certainty what their goals are_

_Fabio, please clarify for me that idea because I don't understand it_ I said.

_I repeat_ he said sententiously, _I want you to understand: religions cannot curb passions, because these are nothing more than instinct; they stem from it and are uncontrollable; they can, in fact, be disguised, but avoided, never. They will survive beyond everything. That's the truth_

_About truth, how to you classify it?_

_Truth exists, but only to the extent of the interest that a person has in defending it. The precise norm of life is a sublime form that some define with the smoothness of a lie. Perhaps misled, we come to such profound or superficial reasoning that we end up asking ourselves: What is real and what is a lie? Actually, the world in which we live is a lie that we take to be true_ he concluded solemnly.

# The Man Who Bought His Own Death

Fabio Estenoz had gotten permission to possess all sorts of firearms, but he was hardly ever armed, except for one time when I caught him in a very pitiful condition. I remember it well: I occasionally passed by the place in the city where we first saw each other; the loud tone of his voice in the little coffee shop was clearly audible in the street. At first I couldn't recognize him, however when I entered, I found him drunk as never before, his eyes fuzzy from the alcohol, wobbly, with a revolver in his right hand and challenging everyone present. I went resolutely to him and disarmed him without his offering the slightest protest. Then I all but dragged him to his car and took him home. His vocabulary, always elegant and meticulous, under the influence of alcohol had become vulgar and coarse, even towards me for whom he said he felt so much affection. This new aspect of my benefactor and friend was completely unknown until then. Such a worrisome splitting of his personality left me bewildered, disappointed, and resentful. Because, even though it is true that many times, when he was warmed by drink, I listened to his opinions about politics and heard him philosophize, never was his condition so alarming to the point of becoming aggressive, uncontrolled, and worse yet, brutal.

The situation of the country made him despair: violence unleashed like a disastrous hurricane; indifferent and merciless assassination; the debased minds of guerrillas; the cold calculation of the underworld; towns destroyed without mercy; peasants massacred, their blood spilled, poured out on the earth that previously had been a sacred gift. All that consumed him.

_And they say we are not at war!_ he was accustomed to commenting frequently.

_There is clamoring for peace, but we all carry this bloody pain like a red-hot iron against our chests. The rivers are polluted, their waters turned into cemeteries by the beasts thirsty for power_

And he continued, anguished: _I don't understand. We do nothing to combat this runaway wave. Where, then, shall we look? What air shall we breathe that is different from this that not only wounds and exasperates, but leads to repulsion?_

_Fabio,_ I replied, _we have to shout peace to the four winds, but everyone is deaf, everyone is mute, everyone is blind! Silence and cowardice reign_

With his eyes moist from almost childlike crying, he continued talking:

_I would like to get out of this apocalyptic world, the prison of this present life. I believe it is a humiliation to continue living, just to look at the lying faces, the sweaty faces of those who make up the wolf packs, of those who hide evil behind flags. This rarified air isn't air; it's a whiplash. This smell of so much innocent spilled blood breaks my heart. The crying of the widows and orphans fills my soul with ashes and clouds. In every capital we are silent and gloomy witnesses. The towns and the peasants are the victims. I listen to the thunderous impact of the bombs made of gas canisters above the little white houses in picturesque villages. I see bell towers flattened, walls tumbled down, the piercing murmuring of the humble people who are fleeing and abandoning everything. I am an actor among the ruins left by the vandals, a passive actor in the face of the extermination of the country. We are all actors in the face of the dispossessed and the destitute. But we have no idea what it means to wander around with the fever of being abandoned, with fear and poverty following, undermining our hopes_

Acting like someone getting a breath of fresh air, he continued:

_Because you can't deny it, we are all prisoners, held hostage within ourselves. The blood that is being spilled in our territory inevitably involves us, marks us, scars us forever. We are pariahs anywhere in the universe. I'm telling you again, you don't know how much I would like to disappear. Life has no meaning for me, even though it seems just the opposite. The happiness that I radiate is a mask that you alone are acquainted with. I mislead everyone with my laughter, with its explosive peals, with my jolly, unworried manner, but there are days when I would like to order someone to kill me_

_Heavens!_ I replied. _Don't say that_ And so as not to give it much importance, I responded almost with indifference:

_You would be the man who bought his own death. Let's be sincere, my friend. Behind that mask of yours, I believe that there is a wealth of sadness. Right?_

_Alfred Medina, never forget what I am about to tell you: sadness is to man as the hurricane to the fields. People take the edge off their sadness, and to do that they invent happiness, surround themselves with friends, try to find in others what they know themselves to have: melancholy and everything that stems from it. People spend their whole lives searching for themselves, but they don't realize it. They search in nature and wisdom, they look for centuries in the infinite of the unknown and in the end all they meet is their sadness. Man is born lost in the chaos of the world and dies without finding himself, powerless in the face of the universe: a machine of time and space, the toy of an unfathomable destiny, of an immeasurable cosmic wind. Sadness is an abyss between heaven and earth, a horror of our very selves. It is grief in the face of the impenetrable!_

It was contradiction and irony to hear a man to whom life had entrusted innumerable privileges talk like this. I am making a record of the multiple moments I spent at the side of Fabio Estenoz, because his words and his opinions cannot fade from my memory.

I forgot to give the details of his apartment: restrained, decorated with exquisite taste; he enjoyed all things of beauty and described them with pride, telling their history, how on numerous trips he had acquired them in the most expensive shops in the world. His favorite spot was the library, in which there was a noticeable bohemian atmosphere: collections of very beautiful masks carved in wood, theater masks, colorful Thai masks, ebony masks with partially closed eyes that exude mystery. On a broad Louis XV table, a complete collection of photographs: his ceremonious grandparents, the day of his parents' wedding; pictures of himself in different places in the world—on the canals of Venice, on the streets of Rome, in the most beautiful spots in France with a beautiful young woman, who he said had been his lover and had taught him the language. From wall to wall, expensive books by the best-known authors in the world. On another table, also Louis XV, the great books of the Conquest of the West, under a large wagon such as the pioneers used. He had a collection of clocks from the colonial grandfather clock with cathedral chimes to the folksy Suisse cuckoo. Hourglasses, a pendulum clock that had belonged to his grandmother and had stopped at 11:30 on who knows what day and year. Candelabra of several styles and sizes that I frequently saw all lighted at the same time with their fine silhouettes standing out in the darkness. Fabio liked to turn out all the electric lights and light up his home with multiple candles. In one corner, a small piano. Next to it, the fireplace, lighted when he was present. On the piano, two faint Tiffany lamps provided a romantic and inviting atmosphere. On the wall, his favorite firearms, shiny and quiet. He loved music and literature and often repeated sentences and passages from famous authors: Joyce, Kafka, Herman Hesse, Shakespeare.

His love life.

I don't think it is being disloyal to comment on some episodes of his love life. I believe that the gathering of the information that I can bring together will be to my benefit. Fabio Estenoz loved women, but always taking into account his method of getting them: on street corners, in shops, anywhere; if any of them noticed his attractive figure, he got into a brief conversation and she ended up in his apartment, sharing his bed. Besides that, he loved calling on the telephone pretty girls who amused him. He had the habit of treating them with great affection. He ended up giving them advice for pursuing a different life, and some ended up being lovers of his with some degree of hope; but Fabio couldn't tolerate a woman for very many hours. When he had gotten what he wanted, he fell into a drunken sleep, lulled by music, and got rid of the current woman, no matter the time or the date. Perhaps he was not able to find himself; he had a thousand faces and disliked them all. He had a thousand voices and listened only to the one inside. Given to loneliness, he clung to liquor that encouraged him to talk with himself, to analyze "fragile" humanity in his own way, and to feel the profound emptiness of those who are misunderstood. He had great adventures in love: seasoned young women, tragic women, young women just starting out, middle aged women who were disillusioned with men, beautiful "empty-headed" women, women... Women! How many filled the empty nights of Fabio Estenoz! If whispers and voices stayed put so we could listen to them whenever we wish, there would not be enough space in his apartment for the sounds of the women who occupied its space. Undoubtedly, the atmosphere would be bursting with laughter, promises, and good-byes. To the beautiful Carolina, to Patricia, to Sandra, to Marcela, to Nadia, and to so many others who never returned, because he never wanted to see them again. On the other hand, he sometimes told me he would like to know a woman who would fill his soul with tenderness, but she never showed up. Perhaps for meeting women, this man put up a protective shield. His "friends" disappointed him. Richard, Fernando, Ricky weren't worthy to occupy space in his world. This man who had everything saw how empty his fields were; when there were days of drinking, he could be seen beaming in his car, or speeding on his bicycle, or striding rapidly when he took long walks; he was dressed neatly, with an artist's originality: well-tailored pants of French corduroy, suede jacket, pastel shirt. He almost always wore extraordinary boots and hat that complemented his figure and personality. His wardrobe was to be envied, extensive, full of handsome and novel garments.

He had a mind that was sharp, fresh, and clever when it came to checking on his accounts and business affairs. He didn't miss anything. He always paid close attention, in spite of the absolute confidence that he showed in me. The cares of daily life built up in his head, and in the evening he returned to the same dangerous paths: the search for something that he himself did not fully understand; a world of mystery surrounded him, overcoming him like the darkness that overcomes the evening; and his unrestrained manner of life kept on; days and months went by, he added names of women in his bustling about, like links on a chain with no end; they gave him caresses and sex that at a certain point was what his ardent and untiring body demanded of him. He often told me about his adventures, with minute details: such as the instance of the extremely beautiful and very young Carolina, only eighteen years old; when she came into his life, she was already embittered, with the indelible scar of incest that pursued her like a ghost.

Nadia shone marvelously with her angelic face and her silken blond hair; Fabio had met her in an elegant clinic in the city, where she was visiting a friend hospitalized there and he, on his part, was visiting a psychiatrist friend who had had a serious accident; their eyes met; he invited her to the café and there in a few hours they realized the great attraction that brought them together. I don't know what sort of magical powers Fabio had for attracting women, like bees to honey; in fact Nadia, with an elegant suitcase, moved into his apartment. She was a girl from out in the country, sweet, with gentle ways, and great class; she inspired great confidence from the moment I met her. Estenoz changed remarkably in her presence: every day he left with enthusiasm to check on his businesses, and he was noticeably happy. Somebody was waiting for him at home. The atmosphere in his apartment became more inviting, scented, filled with flowers and music. I imagined with satisfaction that these two lives were united without further hesitation. Finally my great friend and benefactor was going to feel the love of life. I visited them from time to time, because they requested it insistently. They seemed to be happy. He took pleasure in heaping attention on her, and she accepted it with pleasure.

But one morning Fabio called me urgently and asked me to come immediately to his apartment. It was eight o'clock, and he was walking with great strides in the living room, where the lights were still burning. He was in an elegant dressing gown and tearing his hair with both hands. It was easy to see that he was drunk. He asked me quietly to go into the bedroom and talk with her; he wanted me to intercede and tell him what she was thinking. In spite of the uncomfortable situation, I went to the bedroom. On the bed, reclining on a cushion, she looked listless and sad, with eyes that showed clear signs of her crying.

_Nadia, what a pleasure to see you_ I said, trying to seem unconcerned. _How are you feeling?_

Quietly, as fearing to be heard, she said,

_Very bad, my friend, very bad. I haven't slept the whole night_

_What happened?_ I asked her worried, noticing the large eye bags that made her eyes look even sadder and larger.

_Beginning yesterday_ she told me, _he started drinking liquor very early, until daybreak. I have put up with his behavior without failing to take notice; my friend, I despise liquor. This man is a lunatic, an egotist, and in his own words, there is no one like him or any more distinguished name or family of nobler lineage than his; he treated me like a prostitute and someone mentally unbalanced. He searched my life like a bloodhound, he made me confess my past, and then he began to shout, to sling insults, humiliating comments, names that nobody has dared to call me. He underwent an unbelievable metamorphosis; he was not the 'gentleman' I had known_

_Pardon him_ I said. _You can regulate his liquor and do him a lot of good_

_Friend, I won't be able to do it. I don't love him. No matter how much you suggest it to me, there is no longer any communication between the two of us_

I departed, leaving Nadia with her eyes partly closed, overcome by fatigue from the sleepless night.

I found Fabio calmer, seated on the sofa in the library, drinking liquor. When he noticed my presence, he embarked on a series of comments about Nadia's personality that made me shiver.

_She's a poor crazy woman who has had her head operated on. Behind so much beauty and elegance there is an empty mind. I have failed again! I was mistaken once more. I understand my failure_

I didn't reply, nor did I say anything about what Nadia had told me. I left quietly and with great sadness; days later, he himself told me that he had sent her away; he made her pack her suitcase and he called a taxi for her. Before leaving, she threw many kisses to him from the outside door. All I ever found out about this sweet blond girl was that she had returned to her home in the countryside. Perhaps the mysterious ways and the dangers of the big city, the chaos and the moral collapse, frightened her soul and she sought refuge in her parents' house. Fabio continued his licentious life with an unquenchable thirst for amorous adventures. Stimulated by liquor, he continued his nights of philosophizing. For many of those hours, I tried to be at his side. I took care that his drunkenness not become known to his friends or leak into his business dealings. We kept to ourselves during those difficult hours, in the seclusion of his library, from which the sounds of voices could not escape, no matter how loud they were. I also made sure that he was eating during these periods. In the spacious and well-decorated kitchen of his apartment, I spent many hours preparing his favorite dishes for him, comforting him with my words when he was overwhelmed with crying. Analyzing the past, now so far away, I can be certain that my benefactor had a variety of complicated, disconcerting, and surprising personalities: one day he would be euphoric and peaceful, full of dreams, planning trips to faraway countries he had not yet visited. Other times, his spirits were completely in the cellar with a heartfelt tenacious desire to die. To most people, he was a kind, happy gentleman. He was thrilled by nature because, he said, it gave him peace and clarity. He could identify most of the trees when we went out on excursions on any one of his estates; of the green and the freshness of the trees, he used to say, "I carry them in my heart like a light." On occasions he hugged them, closed his eyes and murmured passionately, "I am very fond of trees; their sap excites me and makes me more vigorous." His knowledge taught me that white acacias bloom in August and September; I learned the difference between the strong Phoenix palm and the voluptuous wax palm. I learned about the walnut and the cedar, sacred trees for the Muiscas. I came to appreciate the beneficial aroma of the eucalyptus, the aquatic strength of the poplar, and the usefulness of the ostentatious castor oil plant dressed in scarlet flowers.

In the rambling through my past with my benefactor, I remember—

It was a weekend. We were in his library and there was heavy rain. The wind was making the beams and the roof creak. Estenoz was drunk, but firmly and with assurance, deliberately and without hesitating, he said to me, fixing his gaze on mine as if seeking to find some reaction in my eyes:

_Alfred, I admit to you that I have on several occasions been in a mental hospital. In two of them, they put me in a straitjacket_

_How's that?_ I asked him, justifiably shocked and clinging to the arms of my chair.

_Yes_ he continued, _exactly as I am saying; I see that you are startled. I've wanted to tell you that for a long time. That idea has been tormenting me frequently. I hope you are not too upset, my dear friend. I am under constant treatment, but my illness is hereditary. Now, what do you say?_

I smiled at him, caught between being nervous and being worried. A chilly breeze of tension and strange pessimism seemed to blow through the closed room. I felt something weighing on my chest. Hesitating a little, I answered him, trying to keep my voice firm and normal:

_You know that I am your faithful friend; you can let go of your fears and seek refuge with me whenever you need it_

Then he took my hands in his tightly in a sign of satisfaction and burst into tears such as I had seldom seen from him. I saw that he was utterly defenseless, as if he were a child. From that moment, I decided to be his mainstay, his strong unwavering pillar. That night he cut down on the liquor and talked inexhaustibly until dawn. He told one story and went on to another. He touched on one topic and then another. It was a long chain that seemed to be suffocating him. With my silence as I listened to him, I encouraged his longing so that his tales would continue uninterrupted. To say something, I asked him—not knowing if he was going to answer:

_What were you feeling when you committed yourself into that asylum?_

_Committed myself? No, they committed me on the orders of the person who at that time managed my finances, as he had done since my parents' death in that horrible air accident that darkened my life forever. Someday I'll share with you the details of that part of my journey, but the truth now is that I manage everything about my existence. Under instructions of that somebody, they seized me savagely by surprise, stormed my apartment, broke down the door, and two tall strong 'attendants' in white coats carried me off half dressed with pushing and shoving. I felt extreme rage. Powerless, I shouted at them, 'Have you no respect for my dignity?' When I tried to defend myself like a wounded pursued beast, they gave me a shot and put me in a straitjacket. Waking up was degrading. I was in a closed room with a single steel window through which I saw the days as overcast even though it was sunny outside. Nothing but anguish filled my heart. The walls were padded so that the inmates could not harm themselves by hurling themselves against them. I never had any intention of doing that. Do myself harm? Never! I needed all my five senses intact to survive that critical stage that I was destined to live, alone and imprisoned. I often recited out loud, in order to keep up my courage, some part of 'If' by Rudyard Kipling:

"If you can keep your head when all about you
Are losing theirs and blaming it on you,
If you can trust yourself when all men doubt you,
But make allowance for their doubting too;
If you can wait and not be tired by waiting,
Or being lied about, don't deal in lies,
Or being hated, don't give way to hating, ...

If neither foes nor loving friends can hurt you...

If you can fill the unforgiving minute
With sixty seconds' worth of distance run,
Yours is the Earth and everything that's in it,
and—which is more—you'll be a Man, my son."

Having recited the fragments soulfully and with a strong voice, Fabio used his hands to dry the tears from his eyes and continued his tale:

_Perhaps to check on my state of mind, now no longer in the straitjacket, they gave me brushes and paints. I mixed reds with greens, yellows with blue, ocher with bronze, and instead of painting demons and beasts as so many crazy people do, I painted a red that gave off color like the sun to fall in rays with auras of light blue and white. I allowed all the light that was in me to be seen and intentionally did not use a bit of black. I sent the doctors and nurses a luminous message of peace that I did not actually feel. Within me there was a lot of turmoil and great sadness caused by my isolation and forced loss of freedom. I took advantage of the extensive library at the asylum and spent time reading famous authors: Fyodor Dostoyevsky, Gabriel D'Annunzio, Ernesto Sábato, Gaston Bachelard, Milan Kundera, Fernando Savater, and, with no hesitation, any book that fell into my hands. I have to admit to you that I admire with deep devotion authors who have had the courage to commit suicide: Stefan Zweig, Ernest Hemingway, Leopoldo Lugones, Virginia Woolf, and also the life and death of that painter whom I love so much—Vincent Van Gogh.

_Friend Alfred, what do you think of all this that I'm telling you? Are you frightened?_

Trying to hide my astonishment, in return I asked him calmly and completely naturally:

_You have kept up psychiatric therapy, right?_

_Psychiatrists? What are they good for? To confuse their patients even more. The most daring unfold before them all their wisdom with mental tricks, searching for the soul in the most deeply hidden ins and outs of childhood. One of them gave me sleeping pills, and when I refused them, telling him of my fear of sinking into unreality, he assured me that it was unimportant because he would take charge getting me out of there. In addition, they put you into hypnotic trances, and at the end, what? Nothing beneficial. The only thing that really happens is that they have emptied your pockets. But I'm not going to judge them because now I think I have found a very young psychiatrist friend, and someday I'll tell you about him_ (He never did.)

I admit that with the passage of time, I became accustomed to the alcoholic deliriums of Fabio Estenoz and to his licentious life, fantastic and feigned. My duty was to watch over him, in spite of the fact that he paid no attention to my reproaches and suggestions, particularly those regarding matters of feminine friendships. Each time we talked he had a new story to tell me about the stupendous woman he had met the night before, or that his friend Richard had phoned him to say that he was sending him a "little present." What actually happened was that an amazingly wonderful girl arrived, saying that she was the gift from his friend. Another time he told me that he had received two charming young girl "friends" and that he had made love to both of them, but that they didn't fill his life. To tell the truth in his own words, "he could stand a woman in his bed only a few hours, but he loved them all and needed them." For his nights of rapture, he sought the ideal woman and never found her. He was soaked in a sickly atmosphere of worldly pleasures. His desire to disappear grew each day, and his feeling of cowardice was intense because of not doing it when he most wished to. I don't know what deep secret of this man's personality has eluded me. He was capable, intelligent, altruistic, a reader, a friend to his friends, noble with the poor, but stubbornly cruel with himself.

A week went by without seeing Fabio. Owing to managing his affairs, submersed in multiple daily tasks, I didn't think about the fact that something serious could have happened to him, since he almost always took care of himself and, besides, requested my company regularly. I set myself to searching the city for him. I went to the places he used to visit from time to time. I cautiously asked various employees at his estates if they knew anything about him, and I always received more or less the following reply:

_Since the boss travels so much, he's hardly ever seen around here_

In his apartment in the capital, his trusted maid Benilda told me:

_I thought that he was on a trip with you_ She followed that up tersely, saying, _If you don't know what's going on with him, who would?_

Thinking for a moment, she exclaimed:

_Have they kidnapped him, since that's so normal in this country?_

_Let's not even think about that_ I answering smiling. _Don't worry, Benilda, I'll come back soon with him_

I left Fabio's apartment deeply concerned about what could have happened to him. I considered going to the police, but with nothing concrete to go on, that would be very serious. Causing a scandal would provoke his anger and discomfort whenever he did appear, brandishing his smile and his self-assurance.

Another week had passed, and Fabio's disappearance was the central concern of my life. Exactly at 7:00 one night there was a special little series of knocks at the door of my apartment. I knew in a moment whose hand was behind them and went to open the door immediately.

_Alfred, you respectable and beloved old man!_
His friendly arms fell onto my shoulders.

_Where on earth were you? You had us seriously worried_ I said.
_Now, my friend, look at me. Don't you notice anything?_

He was dressed completely in black. His voice was at once serious and distressing, his words slow and difficult, as if he were carefully weighing each of them. He sat down and continued:

_My friend the psychiatrist died two weeks ago!_

He ended with his voice almost drowned in sobs.

_I'm lost, completely lost_

He covered his face with his hands, looking desperate. Suddenly, lifting his head towards me, he asked me as a helpless child would do:

_You'll help me, won't you?_

Instantly I replied:

_How foolish to ask me that! I will help you with all my being. Here's my head, and here's my soul_ I said, striking my breast. _Finally I am going to do something for you, to whom I owe so much_

There was deep emotion in the air for a moment, and Fabio, after a long sigh, exclaimed:

_I understood the goodness of your heart, Alfred, from something I saw in your heart on that night long ago. I am so distressed. Look what I wrote last night_ he continued, giving me a small piece of paper with the following written on it:

In a desperate hour of agony / one tries to be in touch with his soul / deep within. / Your chest feels like a dammed up river, / an intense burning, / a flame that scorches the instants, the hours, time itself. / Something intense, shapeless, / a hopeless destiny, an absurdity, an overwhelming solitude. / To penetrate this alien world / is to understand that beneath the skin that covers us, / we find only mysteries./ With chained dreams, / with searing thirst / you seek yourself deep inside./ You find only the dark and agitated wings / of the immense hollow. / In search of the golden fields of grain / we may rip ourselves apart deep within. / Even so, the doors are closed, / the rubble just the same. / A vortex of silence, / not even our voice is ours. / And that face in the mirror is a ghost, / someone unknown shipwrecked / in the unending night of the universe.

Seeing him like that, in agony over the death of his friend, I felt immense pity for the man whose kindness and friendship to me I am unable to express adequately in words. I thought his sorrow was justified. I found what he had written moving, and that night I reiterated my formal promise to stand by him, even if I had to distance myself for a time from his business affairs. My intuition told me that his spirit was very weak. I sensed that he felt abandoned and frustrated. Later, when he was calmer, he interrupted my thoughts with his explanation:

_I won't expand_ he said, _on details about my friend's death. The cruel reality is that he is definitely gone and I survive. Besides, to crown it all off, I'm done for. Take this and read it!_ he said, handing me an envelope.

It contained a beautifully handwritten letter with perfect spelling. But what am I saying? It wasn't a letter, but rather an ominous message that said:

Mr. Fabio Estenoz

City

We are aware of you secret business dealings and your adventures with drugs. We have convincing proof against you and your friend the psychiatrist. Tell us, shall we cause a scandal? Your money can avoid it. At this point, hand over one hundred million pesos. We will wait for you at midnight tomorrow on 56th Street at the corner below the cemetery. You will walk up and I will walk down, so that we will meet at the central gate of the cemetery. I don't need to remind you that if you alert the police, you will die.

(signed)  The Man in Gray

I read and reread this note trying to find some solution. Perplexed and worried by such an abominable anonymous letter, Fabio unexpectedly grabbed the paper from me, tore it in two, and threw it into the flames in the fireplace, where in seconds it was reduced to ashes.

_This is what one does with an anonymous letter, my dear Alfred_ he said with composure and continued, _but I assure you and I swear to you that in spite of the danger implicit in this confrontation, we will triumph!_

He finished these last words in a tone that did not seem to me very convincing.

_You were completely wrong_ I said severely, _to throw into the fire the proof with which we could go to the police. This is nothing but ordinary blackmail. Today they want one hundred million; tomorrow it will be much more. Think this over, please_ I insisted.

_How naïve you are, Alfred! To consider the police! Leave them out of it; they're a bunch of incompetents! Don't you know that the world is full of people who are good for nothing because ignorance is all around us? No country, no government concerns itself with having its people live well, with surrounding them with happiness. Do you believe that if those in charge were not thieves anyone would have to leave the country, anyone would have to go elsewhere to seek happiness and well-being? I'll take care of this my way_ he said forcefully and with contempt.

After a long diatribe about the police and those who govern, he came back to the real matter and in a calmer voice exclaimed:

_You and I alone will face this situation. Or are you perhaps afraid?_ he added sarcastically.

_Me, afraid? To defend you?_ I said, _I know the meaning of the word 'courage.' Please don't make me feel bad_

Then after a short pause, I asked:

_You don't have any idea who this man in gray who signed this miserable piece of junk could be?_

_I'm coming to that, Alfred. These last few nights, as I walked around in the city lamenting the absence of my dead friend, I noticed that a man, of about my height, thin, in a light gray suit, was following me. I know that he has shadowed me a lot, I don't know for how long. But I have felt his presence with increasing intensity_

_And have you seen his face?_ I asked diligently.

_His face? It's useless to try to see it. He undoubtedly hides it deliberately. He wears a gray hat that is always tilted forward_

When that conversation ended, Fabio began smoking, absorbed in his own thoughts. And I undertook the job of pondering this absurd and irrational situation. Little time remained to analyze and take action in the face of the quandary before us. A cold sweat broke out on my forehead, nose, and hands. Affecting calm, I broke the silence:

_We'll take care of this in the best way_ I said firmly, adding, full of courage, _Do you want to sleep or would you like a whiskey?_

_No, Alfred, one can't drink and at the same time face a situation such as the one before us. I will try instead to stay sober, sleep enough, and wake up clear-headed. Tomorrow I'll share with you any other plan that comes to me tonight. And you, you will do likewise?_

_Agreed_ I answered. _Two clear minds can accomplish a lot in the face of a threat like this. I think this blackmail may come from some charlatan. Or it could come from some group of guerillas or from an underworld gang, for all I know_

That night we agreed that Fabio would not go to his apartment. He took my bedroom, and I took the guest room. I didn't manage to sleep. My eyes seemed wounded, kept open by insomnia and worry. Here I am, from one day to the next, foundering on a problem that seems not only serious but murky and uncertain. The main character in a situation that shows signs of becoming either comic or tragic; a valiant soldier who would not be made to desert even by the dizziness of anguish. On tiptoe, cautiously, after having said goodnight to Fabio, I went to observe him. Peaceful, quiet, enviable sleep accompanied him. It was disconcerting. I returned to my bed, and my efforts to calm the anxiety that seized me were fruitless. The man in gray followed every pathway in my mind. I felt his footsteps even in my heart, and his shadow became linked with mine. The bitter ways of my past paraded through my bedroom, pursuing me as I turned over and over again in my bed with my face buried in the pillows. In spite of all the recollections and remembrances, in spite of all the memories that wrapped themselves around my bedroom, in spite of all the troops of people lost in the past who I knew and with whom I was connected, the man in gray always popped up in the shadows of my mind with menacing words. Suddenly I realized the value of time when I heard my alarm clock do its job. If only I could stop time! But what is time? After all, it is man himself marking out the universe, and my clock was my superior when it subjected me to the unavoidable sentence of its untiring, precise, insistent little hands. An overwhelming, cutting cold invaded the blankets on my bed and grabbed hold of me. For a few minutes, that cold, the dawn, the bells, the hubbub erased the despicable figure of the man in gray. I slept for perhaps an hour more, during which I had a dream that I found to be portentous:

I saw a beautiful, delicate woman wrapped in tulle, returning from the past in the fog; a tender, attractive dog accompanied her, and he too was coming from the past. But the past and death were all the same thing. She approached slowly and lightly, put one of her long thin hands on the light switch of my room. I watched her without moving and saw how as she disappeared she left the ends of her fingers on the button. Later, in a social gathering, she joined with many guests, smiling and happy. I went to greet her, but astonishment seized me! The fingers on one of her hands were missing! Seeing my astonishment, she fled quickly and disappeared in the garden. In my dream I discovered regression to the past and how close death is.

The next day, the morning gleamed as recently washed by heavy rain. On the street, the usual sounds of traffic, the usual voices. I felt that time was not normal, that something strange was floating in the air. Things were happening that were a long way from my daily routine. I had a feeling that some very unusual threads were ambushing my universe.

Fabio said good morning, sounding a little worried, which I fully understood. Then I prepared a simple breakfast: coffee with milk, toast and jelly. The telephone rang three times. The first call, at ten in the morning, was from Miss Clara, the main person in the office, to update me on business matters. The other two were, in order, from a man and from a woman, both asking for Fabio. Following his instructions, I said he wasn't there. Later we agreed to disconnect the telephone so we could concentrate on our midnight plan. Estenoz, in addition to being practical, was extremely meticulous. He wanted all our future steps to be sketched out on paper. After a prolonged search, we found a piece of cardboard in one of my desk drawers. (They say that piece of cardboard was not to be found later in my apartment, nor was there the least bit of proof of its existence.)

_Just what we need_ said Fabio when he had it in his hands. _Just exactly what we need for what I have determined to do. Remember what I am going to tell you, Alfred, so that you don't forget it: that damned letter said '56th Street at the corner below the cemetery. You will walk up and I will walk down, so that we will meet at the central gate of the cemetery'_

Immediately he began drawing the area mentioned on the cardboard and drew in the two figures, one going up and one going down, while he continued speaking:

_At midnight the traffic lights will be off, so it will be rather dark. In addition, there is a line of dense bushes that make the area even darker. On one side there are the high brick walls of the cemetery. On the other side of the street the walls of the marble factory provide no point of surveillance. Certainly, beyond a doubt, the man in gray has picked a rather strategic spot_

His eyes were motionless for an instant, framing a deep, bitter expression.

_But, exactly, what is your plan?_ I asked.

A fleeting sparkle crossed his face, and he answered with certainty,

_You will take a taxi to the lower corner of the cemetery on 56th Street. Without rushing, you will begin to walk up the street. Don't forget, the man in gray will come down the street to meet you at the center gate; seeing you, he will think that it is I with the 100 million. The charlatan is going to have a huge trick played on him when we catch him red-handed. That's our main objective. Staying alert, you won't let him make a single suspicious move. If necessary, you will intimidate him with the pistol that you manage so masterfully. I will come along at a distance behind you with the two detective friends who will be accompanying me. How does that suit you? Do you like the ruse or does it give you the shivers? I think what we are going to do is preferable to waiting for the man in gray to attack us sometime or other in our offices, or in your house, or in mine. I repeat, if he makes any move to attack, fire without hesitating. And if you kill him, you will have rid society of an evil extortionist. You won't go to jail, because you will have acted in self-defense. I will bear witness to that, supported by the detectives. Tell me, are you afraid still afraid?_

I made an effort to appear perfectly natural, but my voice was shaking. Nevertheless, with a somewhat unconcerned smile, I answered:

_Fear? No, but if that man in gray is part of a gang of three or four, which is quite likely, I will be in imminent danger of death!_

_Gang? What gang? Don't make more of it than there is. You'll see how unfounded your fears are. Right now you're letting fear get the upper hand and you have become a pessimist. Alfred, please, don't be afraid_

I took a deep breath to gather courage, and I innocently convinced myself that I was taking on a great adventure like those I organized with my young friends when I was a child. I let him go find the detectives, since according to what he said he had an appointment set up with them. We agreed to meet again in my apartment at 6:00 in the evening.

At noon I was in the Belgian restaurant trying to have lunch. When I finished the dessert and coffee, I was greatly surprised to find myself unable to detect any flavor whatsoever on my palate. Nor did I have any recall of the meal I had been served. I had eaten like an automaton, meditating second by second on those crucial hours that were approaching. At 12:00, precisely at that hour, I would go to sacrifice myself like cannon fodder for my friend and benefactor. My thoughts didn't leave me in peace. What if I had to kill the blackmailer? The sweet tones of my mother's voice came to mind again:

_Remember the Ten Commandments—"thou shalt not kill; thou shalt love thy neighbor as thyself"_

Sweat and uncontrollable shaking ran through my body. To reject the plan, which more than a plan was an order and furthermore an urgent request from my friend, would be to lower myself greatly in his esteem. Showing cowardice, completely shameful. To make him change the plans and not show up for the meeting that night? Impossible. Stubbornness and the grandeur of his plans were characteristic of him. It was difficult to dissuade him when he had a clear plan in mind. Where to seek assistance? A break in trust could seriously complicate matters. I should do nothing to put my benefactor in danger. Ten, twenty, I don't know how many cigarettes my lips sucked on. My fingers were red from wringing my hands so much. My fingernails dug into my flesh in a fit of terror! What if time stood still and Fabio were run over by a car! A car, that's it! In front of me, the insistent sound of a horn made me realize that I was no longer in the restaurant but in the middle of the street. The irate words of the driver comforted me because they shook me back to awareness: "Beast!

Animal! Dummy!" shouted the driver. I just smiled innocently and perhaps convinced him that his words were unjust, because he was looking at an imbecile or an escaped lunatic on the street.

It was 3:00 in the afternoon when I got to the Café Gloria. I had to look for somewhere to sit in a hurry so I could give my body a rest and let my thoughts turn to looking for a solution to my serious problem. Like someone lost in a dark labyrinth and turning this way and that, my poor mind went round and round without finding a way out. I drank several small cups of coffee. Suddenly a friend was in front of me—friend X, so as not to put him in any danger.

_Hello, Alfred_ he said with enthusiasm. _I almost didn't recognize you. It's been so long since I've seen you, buddy!_

He gave me a big hug and began to run on at the mouth. I let him talk as much as he wanted, and I acknowledged him with slight nods and an occasional monosyllable.

_So, you're getting along splendidly, eh? And you work with that millionaire Estenoz? Congratulations, because it pays to hang out with the right people_

Either because of the extreme pallor of my face or because of my indifference to his words, or because he was in a hurry, what happened was that my friend took his leave almost immediately, saying:

_Goodbye, dear Alfred. But don't be a stranger. I come here almost every night. We could talk about business_ He gave me a pat on the back and acting important while putting his fingers together, he ended by saying:
_ There are piles of opportunities!_

When he had left, my spirit followed him shouting:

_Save me, save me! Advise me, help me! If you only knew!_

But my cowardly body was glued there, seated at the table of an ordinary café, mummified, like a puppet with a broken string.

A sharp little voice came into my ears:

_Sir, a small coin for a bit of bread_ He held out his grubby little right hand with dirty fingernails. His little body swayed back and forth, and he exclaimed,
_I'm hungry!_

That poor little beggar child, shorter than the café table where I was sitting, fixed his shining sad eyes on me.

_Oh, poor child!_ I said to myself. _How much I would give to be able to hide myself in your poor rags! How much I would give to be you and enjoy the gentle freedom of the poor!_

My beleaguered heart was carried away by those hungry shining eyes, by the enviable serenity of that ragamuffin, and I asked the waitress to serve him coffee and milk, bread, and eggs. When I had paid the bill, I left feeling a hint of optimism and lost myself among the people who were crossing the street. There was a carnival atmosphere in the city. I don't remember why, but a lively man who was not completely unpleasant came up to me on the street and very agilely brought me up to a booth, put a shotgun in my hands, and said:

_Try your luck, sir, for just a few pennies. Try it, please!_ And then in a louder voice, he began to say:
_The gentleman is going to try his luck. Another one taking aim. Gather around, everyone!_

In front, against a wall, a pile of packs of imported cigarettes, like a tempting prize for someone who made a good shot. The man continued shouting, and I raised the weapon mechanically, observed the shadow of the man in gray on the wall, my hands trembled, and boom! The shot went into the floor causing the rascal and some other people to laugh at what they took to be something amusing, unaware of the circumstances that were weighing on me.

I roamed through many streets, entered and left several shops, mixed in with people who were in a hurry, looked at bookstore windows without daring to do anything in particular. I wandered around the city for I don't know how many hours.

At 6:00 on the dot, Fabio and I were in my apartment. As night fell, with unusual joy and enthusiasm (I now think it was a diabolical enthusiasm), he said with emotion in his voice:

_Everything is falling into place, my friend. I now have the two detectives I talked to you about. Look at them unobtrusively. They are at the corner_

He drew the curtains with great care and presented them to my eyes. It was evident that down there two well-dressed men were scanning the balconies of my apartment. For a long time they paced back and forth as if waiting for a call.

_Do you see?_ he said. _Do you feel calmer protected by the detectives that you have seen and verified?_

The truth is that the presence of those two men gave me courage. I felt that the required plan to which my fate was submitting me was strengthened, had a chance to succeed.

Meanwhile, Fabio, with an open book, was killing time in the corner of the living room. He smoked one cigarette after another. He gave the impression of complete tranquility, of unusual self-assurance, of impassive recklessness. He enjoyed a whiskey with pleasure and delight. I pondered the situation as those who are condemned to death must do. I counted the hours and the minutes, filling them with recollections. I reviewed the memories and secrets of my soul. I brought together all the roads I had travelled into a single crossroads. Later, he abandoned his book and I my thoughts. We gave ourselves over to brief comments and practicing the task we would carry out at midnight.

He said over and over:

_Remind yourself again. You will leave at 11:30 at night for the corner of 56th Street at the lower part of the cemetery. You will walk slowly up so as to give time for the man in gray, the detectives, and me. When you see him, raise the briefcase in your left hand to give him confidence. With your right hand, you will have a firm grip on the pistol. Have no fear; the two detectives will fire if they see you in trouble_

That night, 11:30 struck cold on the wall clock. The chimes were an alert, a premeditated message. I felt that everything around me was strange. A stupor invaded the depths of my soul. Fabio got up from the couch ceremoniously and with emotion, gave me a tight hug, and said in a trembling voice:

_Neither you nor I will ever forget this! Alfred, I will owe you my life!_ he said seriously.

Afterwards, with urgency, almost unexpectedly, he put in my hands a briefcase that I had never seen before. My innocence and my faith in Fabio were such that it didn't occur to me to open it. Everything happened so quickly, with no time for doubts. Besides, with the rush and fear that seized me, I took it, felt that it seemed lighter than I had imagined, and left in a hurry without further comment. I left Fabio with the same unconcerned appearance and serving himself a new glass of whiskey.

The cold wind that night struck against my face. What if the man in gray didn't exist, what if everything were a classic drama, what if we were playing as when we were children! What if time would stand still! What if nature came to my rescue and there were an earthquake like the one I lived through uninjured in Caracas! What if I had a heart attack! Night advanced and my hand stopped an old Chevy driven by a thin harsh man about fifty years old:

_Please, 56th Street at the corner below the cemetery_

In the taxi, my thoughts continued: Why didn't I stumble onto a driver who was one of those pirates who attack the passengers and who are so numerous these days? Why didn't they mug me and rob me? Why? Why? The driver looked at me insistently in the rearview mirror and saw that my face seemed to be impassive. What do you suppose this fifty-year-old man might think of me? He tried to chat with me, but I avoided it firmly. The streets we drove along were dark and deserted, traffic lights blinking on some of them. As the taxi went along, I felt an immense desire to be in a wreck. What a good opportunity it would have been to come out well from such a situation! But not even that was likely because there were so few cars out at that hour. Like an automaton when we arrived at my destination, I paid what was on the meter and got out, almost in slow motion. The driver was in no hurry to leave. Would he have thought I looked like a bank robber? Would he have suspected that something

wasn't right about me? Would it have intrigued him
that there was a man with a briefcase so late at night
on such a silent and sinister corner? What a confused
jumble of thoughts tortured me! I waited until the taxi
had finally started off and was lost from view several
blocks ahead. I began my ordeal. I looked behind and to
the sides—just shadows and trees like ghosts. The walls
of the cemetery had never looked higher or gloomier.
I had never felt myself immersed in such mystery and
confusion. Absolute silence. I picked up my pace. No,
I mustn't hurry. I was still a few blocks from my goal.
My wristwatch said 11:55. Weariness was eating at my
heart. Sweat was pouring down my forehead. So I was a
few yards from the cannon and minutes from eternity.
I no longer knew what I was thinking. But, yes, I was
thinking that what would interest the man in gray most
was the briefcase. I could leave it for him and take off
running. But for Estenoz, what was important was to
catch the man and be rid of him. That last thought
caused me to shudder. An old, tall, wan stray dog passed
by me, raised his leg and urinated calmly on one of the
trees. He went on up the street in a hurry, as if someone
were waiting for him.

As for me, I felt more unfortunate and even ridiculous.
A dog wandering around knew where he was going,
was free, had come close to me and was so unconcerned

that he didn't even sniff me, not bothering to investigate that man alone in the night. By contrast, I was adrift, worse off than that stray dog, the puppet of someone crazy who was gambling with my life. How on earth had I accepted this challenge? The famous statement of a friend came to mind: "I go with my friends as far as the grave, but I don't allow myself to be buried with them."

I paused next to a tree, almost leaning on it, and put the briefcase down. I was getting ready to react to that absurd situation when, in the distance, I saw someone and then heard the footsteps coming down the street in the same direction. I picked up the briefcase again and stayed by the tree, fixed and petrified. No room for doubt, there is someone, it's not a ghost, it's a person, and when it came closer I could see it was a man! It was all I could see.

Midnight struck, I don't know where. Oh, if bells only had eyes the way they have sound! That man, would I allow him to come closer? How much closer? My heart was beating faster and the footsteps kept coming... They kept coming... Waves of heat and cold tortured my face. Sweat was running down my forehead, and I felt that in my throat not speaking was increasing the saliva and that it made a dry sound as it passed through. I was trembling surrounded by the night. With my left arm I lifted the briefcase to the level of my shoulders... and the man kept coming and... he kept coming. Now with slow steps, in a catlike dance. I saw that there was something shiny in his hands and that unavoidably he was coming towards me... the light was dim, shadows crossed one in front of another before my eyes... my panic and my confusion and my instincts were stronger than my makeshift courage, more powerful than my commitment to my friend and ... I fired. Having lost control of myself, I fired. A body fell on the pavement a few yards from me; I felt it hit. Afterwards, silence, the terrifying stillness of everything. I tried to run, but my legs were heavy, motionless, stuck to the ground. In the whole lonely street, nothing indicated the presence of anything. I had no intention of getting any closer to the one who was down because that could be a trick to do me in.

Suddenly a police car appeared, then two, and three, and four, with their shrill sirens and their flashing red lights. Several policemen got out and went to what was on the ground. Others handcuffed me and shouted loudly:

_Alfred Medina is under arrest for murder!

_No, please, officers, Fabio Estenoz will come, and he'll explain everything_ I said almost in a voice that I thought was convincing.

_Fabio? How cynical, how impertinent!_ exclaimed one of them in ironic tones. And casting a contemptuous look in my direction, he said:

_So Fabio will explain everything?_

He bent me down. He shone a bright light on a body.

How can I explain the horror and the astonishment of those moments! I felt as if I were fainting, as if air weren't getting to my lungs, as if I were living in a nightmare. Dante's inferno, the explosion of the atomic bomb in Hiroshima, the attack on the Twin Towers in New York were small matters in comparison to what I was experiencing.

A spine-chilling scene: a slow, fatal trickle of blood was running out of that forehead; an ironic smile of satisfaction and jubilation, I wouldn't say dying, was resplendent on those lips; the pale face radiated happiness. The body spread out on the pavement looked like a sacrificed god. That body, still warm, was ... the man in gray... And that man in gray was ... Fabio Estenoz!

Enveloping circles of yellow and red danced before my eyes. A thousand screams squeezed together in my throat... Soft shrill whistles assaulted my ears... Anguish disfigured me... I felt my body shaken by waves that racked and sank me—waves that came and went, and nothing more. In my contorted face, my eyes burning like embers longed to release torrents of crying, but the tears remained congealed.

I killed the good man, the philosopher, the benefactor, Fabio Estenoz, who did not love life, who desired and loved death but couldn't manage it. I killed the person who, irrationally, almost unbelievably, had only one intention: that it would be I who ended his life!

Twelve long months have passed. In their way and with huge headlines, the press publicized the matter:

> "Alfred Medina killed his patron with premeditation. There is trustworthy data that the day before the crime Fabio Estenoz had requested the service of two detectives because he feared that his administrator would make an attempt on his life. Unfortunately, when they arrived on the scene, the crime had already been committed, with additional problem that Mr. Estenoz had called them at 11:30 at night requesting that they be with him an hour later. A briefcase with a hundred million in cash, a passport, and a ticket to travel to Spain the next day were found in Medina's possession."

Others wrote: "Each month Alfred Medina diverted enormous amounts to his account, and it is said that he had a strong box in one of the city's banks." Soon someone even more audacious came up with a story suggesting that we were lovers. Words, words that the heartless, irresponsible press uses to pass judgement on humanity. They don't care about the harm caused by their commentaries, their poisonous stings, their caustic opinions.

Much libel and many lies have been written about the event. Only now do I see clearly in the darkness of my life!

Fabio Estenoz, the man in gray, the one who bought his own death. Fabio Estenoz, "my future," as he said repeatedly, diligently tried to find in me the birthplace of his eternity, molded my thoughts, conformed my spirit to his very subtly while deceiving everyone— and, what is most terrible, deceiving me, his "victim." He was a psychopath, a man who had a clearly defined goal—the obsession to die. But incapable of doing it with his own hands, his unhealthy astuteness and his intelligence led him to train me for his unwholesome purposes. Long months have passed, and I still can't understand how that multifaceted, clever man ensnared me so completely in his life, and I don't understand how I could spend so much time with him without noticing the danger that was stalking me. I don't want to tarnish his name, the name of the one who did me so much good. We have both been the playthings of a terrible fate. We were carried along by the same slippery, rotten current. The reality is that he is submersed in his desired fate, he has come to the fulfillment of his ambition, and I unluckily float and survive. From the greatest depths within me grief constantly gnaws at me, leaves me shattered. Convicted with no way out, with every path blocked, tears and sobs exhausted.

I feel my cowardly hands on my body, as if they were two vile hooks trying to hide their shame. I despise every one of their nerves, every one of their veins and their nails that I have intentionally let get long and black like those of animals. The wrinkles of my joints that look like little rivers of blood, the dark dry skin of these hands is like alligator skin—repulsive. I detest my hands, indirect accomplices, because if they did not exist my breast would not now be destroyed, nor would it be acquainted with the bitter taste of remorse. I curse my feet, for if I didn't have them, they would not have taken me that fatal night towards the abyss in which I feel myself eternally buried. I despise myself totally and absolutely!

I want to disclaim my parents' family name, because through me their virtue has been diminished and their memory vilified by the cruelty of abundant erroneous comments.

May the earth mercifully cover their mortal ears so that my defamed name does not disturb their physical disintegration!

Balzac has said it: "The only thing that is ever complete is misfortune."

Mine is total, full to the brim and overflowing with incalculable bitterness! To whom can I turn? Who are my witnesses?

I await the verdict calmly. Let them judge me, and as the saying goes: "To judge a person, it is necessary, at the very least, to be aware of his secret thoughts, of his misfortunes, of his feelings. To seek nothing in his life but the events in concrete order is to make of his chronology the tale of fools."

Cruel, implacable circumstances condemn me! But I carry something within me that I had left out and that no one knows. I believe in Almighty God! Omnipotent! Who judges everything and sees everything! The God of my parents and of my ancestors! He knows that I am the victim of the man who bought his own death!

# ABOUT THE AUTHOR
# BERTHA LOPEZ GIRALDO

She was born in Manizales (Colombia). She was educated in the capital of Caldas and at the end of her studies travelled throughout the country and overseas performing poetry recitals. Besides a poet, Bertha is a declaimer. She studied reciting and dramatic arts at the Teatro Colón in Bogotá where she performed several times.

She is also an interior decorator and has successfully practiced this profession in Caracas, Venezuela where she lived for 28 years. She now resides in the US and writes a weekly column for the Spanish Journal in Milwaukee, WI.

Bertha has been included in the following anthologies:

"Women in Colombia"
"Feminine Values in Colombia"
"Goddesses in Bronze" by TeresaRozo, 1995.
"ABC of Literature in Great Caldas" by Adel López Gómez.
"Current Poetry of Caldas" from the Caldas Culture Institute, and "Who is who in Colombian Poetry" by Rogelio Echevarría.

Published Books:

"Poems of rain and snow"poetry; "This is my body Love" poetry; "The Silence of the Dogs"memoir, and "The man who bought his own death", novel.

Unpublished Works:

"Under the skin", poetry. "Intimacy paths", poetry. "Clouds of sand", poetry. "Gertrude", novel.

# CONCEPTS

## BERTHA LOPEZ GIRALDO, AN INTELLECTUAL TREASURE

*The Man Who Bought His Own Death* is not only a beautiful book but also an indispensable book, one of those that send up flares and indicate paths. Bertha López Giraldo, the author of this book that is more intense than lengthy, fully meets the requirement of Julio Cortázar: "A good novel, in order to captivate the reader, must be incisive and unremittingly trenchant from the very first sentences." *The Man Who Bought His Own Death* was written with restrained inspiration, with controlled fire, with overflowing spiritual strength. Good narrative must not become lost in social or literary digressions nor in detailed descriptions of places or situations. When the story is burdened with descriptive elements, with affected expressions, it borders on the form appropriate for a local color article. The good narrator tames the hurricane of the passions and subjects it to an agreeable temperature, to a gradual unfolding, keeping the reader's interest alive until finally leaving one in peace at the end of the novel. And that is what happens in the novel of Bertha López Giraldo.

The very few characters in *The Man Who Bought His Own Death* are strong, well drawn psychologically, and always move in a scene filled with suspense. The work is concise, lively and elegant, with a fine spirit of observation. Control and good taste stand out. Bertha López has insatiable intellectual curiosity and is always working with the same ease, whether in poetry or prose. She is idealistic, tolerant, and cultivates an optimistic and warm way of thinking. I admire Bertha López because she is an intellectual from head to toe. She's a prestigious figure in the field of letters. I respect the strength of those who work in the field of the humanities. There is sweat hidden behind a poem, a short story, a tale, a sculpture—a kind of fatigue, of crystalized sacrifice. Together with food, love, and friendship, art is the most necessary part of daily life. Only art stimulates existence. It is true that the sun, the moon, and the stars are something miraculous. But what shall we say about music, poetry, good prose, painting, sculpture? The artist is a manufacturer of happiness, a distributor of emotions. Let us recall the greatest orators, the works that we always return to and that please us so much. The artist is a powerful developer of emotions and contributes to our attachment to life.

About Manizales, it was once said: It is a city of 200,000 poets and a few others. Almost everyone there speaks Latin. Well, then, Bertha López Giraldo was born in that prestigious city. She was a reciter at an early age, and her poetry circulates in several anthologies. She is the author of *Poemas de lluvia y nieve / Poems of Rain and Snow, Este cuerpo es mi Amor / This Body Is My Love*, and the beautiful story *El silencio de los perros / The Silence of the Dogs*, also available in English. Other high-quality works of hers, "Nubes de arena / Clouds of Sand" and "Gertrude" await publication. Established critics have praised her personal output. Bertha López, no matter what anyone says, no matter the genre, is always the same—fulsome and resonant, inspired and well spoken. In the novel *The Man Who Bought His Own Death*, Bertha López Giraldo doesn't get lost in stylistic concerns, as if she were the daughter of thunder. Her story is clear and limpid, flowing like a brook through the meadow. The descriptions are brief, as they should be, but fragrant, fresh, and agile.

Choosing something to read is like choosing friends; one as much as the other earns a place in our life and in our emotions. And the novel of Bertha López entertains, enriches, stimulates, and keeps one alert from beginning to end.

Horacio Gómez Aristizábal is an outstanding jurist and member of the Academy of History and of the Academy of Jurisprudence of Colombia. He lives in Bogotá, Colombia.

## A DRAMATIC STORY

After her two beautiful books of poetry, *Poemas de lluvia y nieve / Poems of Rain and Snow* and *Este cuerpo es mi Amor / This Body Is My Love,* and the successful fictionalized story *El silencio de los perros / The Silence of the Dogs,* poet Bertha López Giraldo is now publishing a short novel, *El hombre que pagó su propia muerte / The Man Who Bought His Own Death.* It is a new facet of her intellectual personality and of her literary efforts. In it she proves herself to be a narrator but principally an analyst of the mysterious ins and out of the human soul.

The novel is the story of just two characters: Alfred Medina and Fabio Estenoz, joined, more than in friendship, by the enveloping fascination that the latter exercises over the former, until he succeeds in controlling him completely. If it were a matter of a sexual relationship, one could use the terms incubus and succubus, but it is not this but rather the psychological control that the more astute and persuasive one effects over the more innocent and malleable one in order to get him to commit the most atrocious of actions.

The author gives a physical description of Alfred:

> Failure and disillusionment were seen in his body and in his face; his clothing was beyond old, ragged with the genuine shine of having been washed and ironed too many times; his uncut hair as well as his sickly pallor and poet's beard gave him a favorable look to the eyes of someone who would change his destiny.

He contrasts with the other character in the novel, who is described in this way:

> Fabio Estenoz was good looking, pleasant, very mannerly, with an overwhelming personality, a characteristic of those who move in wealthy high society; he enjoyed making friends without regard to social standing. He went around to bars, frequented clubs sharing smiles and making friends. His thirty-eight years

were a testimony to the life that he seemed to love dearly. Under that pleasant tone of his voice, the hours slipped by happily and peacefully.

From this unforeseen circumstance in the bar, there arises a work relationship and then a friendship between Fabio and Alfred, although, truth be told, the job was a trick to subordinate him and the friendship a trap to lead him to perverse ends. Not only this. Fabio was or is a psychopath, a fan of liquor, under whose effects he shifts and exchanges his usual euphoria, as the author says, for disillusionment, boredom, and nostalgia. He had everything, but in truth he had nothing because he was obsessed with the fear of living, while at the same time lacking the courage to kill himself. He was or is the kind of person who is captivated by the idea of death. He often rambles on about literature, art, religion, trips, politics and society, without failing to mention the innumerable lovers he has taken to bed.

The novel describes a variety of surroundings: bars, luxurious apartments, gloomy streets, estates with lush vegetation, stifling jails. And conversations between the two characters on the most varied topics are recorded. All of it contributes to creating an atmosphere that is varied and, underneath it all, charged with tragedy.

It is a tense and dramatic story, written in simple and transparent style.

In her person, Bertha López Giraldo offers a variety of facets. She is a reciter of poetry, a poet, a novelist, an interior decorator, a promotor of culture, a student of literature (especially in Spanish and English), an intelligent traveler in different countries (in two of which, Venezuela and the United States, she has lived extensively). But her outlook and spirit are essentially Colombian.

Héctor Fabio Varela is a lawyer, a member of the Royal Language Academy, a poet, an outstanding journalist with the daily *Occidente*. For several years he has lived in Santiago de Cali, Colombia.

CPSIA information can be obtained
at www.ICGtesting.com
Printed in the USA
BVHW031429200619
551546BV00001B/2/P